# Gina and the Marines

by

# Gentleman

# Jim

# (James Roberts)

This book is dedicated to:

My amazing cousins who bravely face the challenges of Cystic Fibrosis every day.


My Father and my Uncle who were both Marines.


And the real Gina.

05
I'm glad you three volunteered.
I have a special assignment for you.

16

It's ok mom, I'll be alright. Don't worry.

19

And the award for our toughest Marine goes to: Miguel!

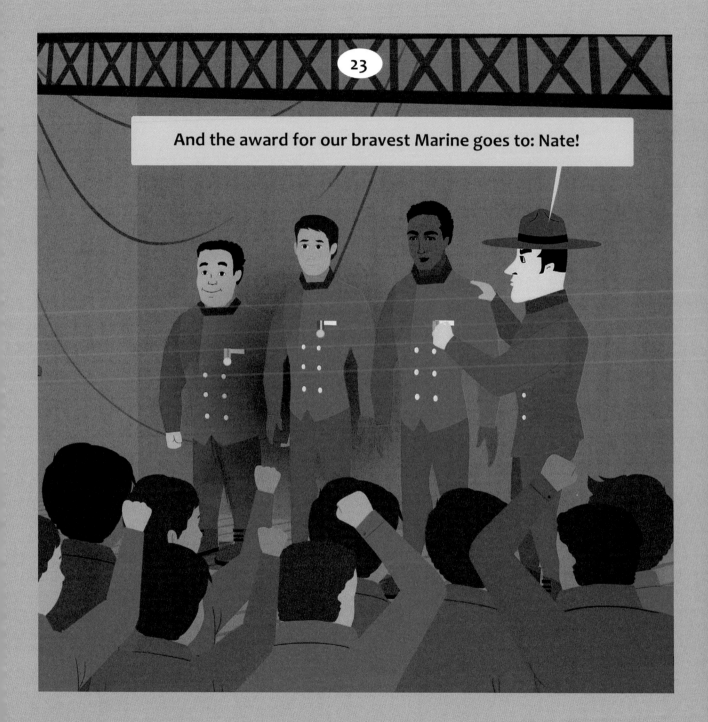

And I want you to have my medal too Gina,
because you're the toughest person I've ever met.

And I want you to have my medal too Gina,
because you're the bravest person I've ever met.

If you enjoyed this book, help spread the word!

*Like our Facebook page: The Little Book About BIG Words

*Follow us on Instagram: authorgentlemanjim

*Visit our website: Authorgentlemanjim.com

Or consider taking a moment and writing a review for us at Amazon.com or Goodreads.com

Thank You!!

# Other books by Gentleman Jim:

The Little Book About BIG Words 1-6

The Little Book About FUN Words 1 and 2

The Thrill Seekers

The Little Book of Sayings

Special Thanks to:

Brenda Van Niekerk

For formatting this book

For publication.

(Brenda@triomarketers.com)